Katy AND THE CHRISTMAS CUPID

A Lake Sterling
Romance

AMY SPARLING

Katy

It's December, but I wake up so toasty warm you'd think it's the middle of summer. Being a twenty-six-year-old who lives with her grandmother has a lot of perks, like getting first dibs on her famous chocolate chip cookies and being able to stay here in my hometown of Sterling, Texas where rental properties are next to impossible to find. Our charming little town is small, and no one ever seems to move out. Plus, I love my grandma a lot, so living here with her is great... most of the time.

She's a thin, tiny woman in her eighties and she's always cold. So when winter rolls around, she cranks the heater up like the walls are made of gingerbread and she's trying to bake them. She also keeps the massive fireplace in the living room filled with a roaring fire. And she'll still wear a cardigan and cuddle up with a blanket on the couch.

I kick out of my sweaty bed sheets and then jump in the shower, keeping the water cooler than usual just so I can remember what being cold feels like. Then I get dressed for work. There is no dress code at Zee Cycles, especially for me, an accountant who works in the offices that are so far away from the main showroom that no one ever ventures in to see me. I could show up in my pajamas and I doubt anyone would know.

But I don't. I wear a pair of dark wash skinny jeans, brown faux-leather boots, a Christmas sweater, and my adorable glass earrings that look like little Christmas light bulbs. I love Christmas, but I have been dreading this week. I have the work holiday party this weekend and then our family Christmas party next week. All of my extended family gets together to celebrate, and this year my remaining three single cousins all got married. Two are pregnant. Leaving me, Katy White, the loser of the family with no spouse, no fiancé, not even a boyfriend.

And while I wish I could say all of the attention will be on my cousins, meeting their new spouses, talking about their future kids, I know without a doubt that most of the attention will go to me.

Everyone will ask why I'm still single. When am I going to settle down? When am I going to leave the tiny town of Sterling and find a *real* job and start a family?

Bah humbug.

Of course I want all of those things. To be perfectly honest, I always thought I would have them by now. I thought I'd meet a wonderful man in college and get married after graduation and have a couple of kids and a nice house and live happily ever after. But all I found in college was an accounting degree. Still, I love my job. Zee Cycles is a rugged motorcycle shop with only one other female employee—my best friend Ari, but it's a good place to work. I'm paid well, and my office is way in the back where no one besides Ari ever goes. If I worked at some high-rise building in the city, I'm sure I'd meet more men each day, which is one of the reasons my parents think I should move to Houston with them. But I love Sterling, and I don't plan on leaving.

After dabbing on some mascara and lip gloss, I head into the extra-warm kitchen and grab some coffee. Grandma sits at the kitchen table sipping coffee from her favorite *World's Best Grandma* coffee mug and reading the news on her iPad. I bought the device for her last Christmas, and she loves it. She takes it everywhere she goes and reads eBooks on it at the doctor waiting room, and watches YouTube videos about knitting and cooking. She calls herself a hipster. I'm not entirely sure she knows what that means.

"What's this fancy thing?" Grandma asks, tapping the envelope on top of a stack of mail. "Please tell me we don't have to go to yet another boring wedding."

I pick it up, noticing the Zee Cycles logo on the outside. My boss, Bruce, went all out this year, ordering those extremely fancy invitations with thick cardstock and shimmery paper and embossed lettering. I roll my eyes as I open it up and read it aloud to her.

"We've been cordially invited to my work's annual holiday party," I say with a snort, setting the invitation down on the table. "I don't know why he sent them to the employees. I obviously know about the party because I have to help decorate the pavilion."

"The pavilion?" Grandma says, looking at the invitation. "The one at the lake?"

I take a sip of coffee. "Yep."

"Doesn't Bruce usually have the holiday party at your work?"

"Yep," I say again. "This year he's inviting all the bigwigs from the motorcycle companies. Like Harley Davidson's executives and stuff. He wanted an even fancier party than usual so he rented out the pavilion." I roll my eyes. "But the food should be good. He's getting real catering, not just ordering a bunch of burgers from Roger's Diner this time."

"It says you can bring a plus one," Grandma says, tapping the invitation with her fingernail. "Who is the lucky gentleman who gets to be your date?"

"You."

"Me?" She chuckles, placing a hand to her chest. "I am not a gentleman."

"No, but you're going to be my date."

She scoffs. "I won't be your date, Katy. You need to find a real date. This seems like a perfect opportunity to invite a handsome young gentleman to spend the evening with you."

I try not to laugh. Handsome? Young gentleman? Those don't exist around here!

"Grandma... I don't know anyone like that."

She presses her lips together in this sassy, sarcastic way. I prefer when she gives this look to my cousins when they've said or done something wrong. I do not like it directed at me.

"There are plenty of handsome young men out

there, Katy." Her expression softens and she looks at me now with something like pity. "You just have to get out of your shell and go find them."

The worst part is that she's right. I am in a shell, in a way. I go to work each day and then come home. Sometimes I'll take a walk around the lake while listening to podcasts, and sometimes Ari invites me to dinners with her boyfriend, where I end up feeling like a third wheel. But I never really get out to meet anyone. And maybe that's the problem.

In the movies and fairy tales, a handsome, perfect man just appears for the heroine to find. They usually meet in some adorably silly way. Like she's walking to class carrying a bunch of books and she trips and the books fall everywhere, and she's flustered and then—bam—Mr. Handsome kneels down and helps her pick up the books. He grins at her, and she grins back, sheepish and shy, and she pushes her hair behind her ears and apologizes and he says it's fine, and then there's this adorable moment where they look into each other's eyes and you know they've just fallen in love.

Yeah, well real life doesn't happen like that.

I'm not going to just plow right into the perfect man on the sidewalk. Sterling is such a small town it doesn't even have sidewalks.

CHAPTER 2

Cody

I love the weather this time of year. I live in Texas, where it doesn't exactly snow, so the winters are cool but not frigid. December is perfect. It's cool enough that we don't have to blow fans in the shop, but not so cold that you're shivering while working on a motorcycle. I wish every month was like this.

Bruce has a rule for all of his employees at Zee Cycles. We have to park way in the back of the facility so we don't take up any good parking spots that are for customers. The motorcycle shop has been in Sterling for fifty years, and it's grown and transformed over the decades. Bruce has a black and white photo of his original building, a small metal shack that only sold bikes and nothing else. Now, the main showroom is a massive metal building with shiny varnished concrete floors and a couple hundred motorcycles, dirt bikes, and all-terrain vehicles all on display under the bright lights. Behind the main warehouse is a large concrete outdoor showroom for the used bikes for sale. Then, way beyond that, across the gravel parking lot, is the mechanic shop where I work. There's a great area on the side of the building, tucked out of the way, that would be a perfect place to park my truck, but Bruce has rules and I follow them because this is a great job.

I get to do what I love with little to no oversight because I'm good at what I do. My phone is vibrating nonstop on the drive to work, and when I park in the employee parking area and start making the trek to my workshop, I check my phone to see what all the fuss is about.

It's the family group chat. They're going on and on about Christmas dinner and who is bringing each dish, and what presents the kids want. I've been assigned to bring napkins and beer. I guess they don't trust me to cook anything, which is probably a good judgment on their part. If it's not on the grill, I'm not exactly good at it.

My seven nieces and nephews range in age from newborn to ten, and I don't need to read the texts about what they want for Christmas because I've already gotten them the best gifts ever. What I lack in cooking skills I make up for in being an incredible gift-giver. They love Uncle Cody. I love them, too.

"Agh—ow!"

I stop, having suddenly slammed into something. Or some*one*, more like it.

"I'm so sorry," I say, holding out my hand to steady the woman in front of me. Her name is Katy, I think. She works in the office.

I was paying so much attention to my texts that I hadn't noticed her walking right toward me. But her phone is in her hand too, so maybe she was doing the same thing.

"It's my fault," she says, rubbing her arm. "I was looking at my phone." She brushes her hand over her head, smoothing down any stray brown hairs that may have come loose from her low ponytail. Seeing her up close like this, I realize she's probably closer to my age. For some reason, I had assumed the office girl was like fresh out of high school or something.

"I was looking at my phone too," I say, holding it up with a sheepish grin. "Guess it's both of our faults. Are you okay?"

She nods, then narrows her eyes as she looks at my phone. "Oh my gosh... that thing is horrible! How do you even see through all those cracks?"

I shrug, glancing down at the phone in my hand. It's been dropped a few times around the workshop and the screen is mostly shatters by now. "I don't use it very often. Plus, I can still read the texts."

She lifts an eyebrow. "You really need a new phone."

"Nah," I say, "They're expensive."

She puts a hand on her hip. "I've seen your paychecks. You can afford a new phone."

"You've seen my paychecks?" I say, confused and weirdly fascinated.

"Of course. I see everyone's paychecks."

"Why?"

She stares at me like I'm dumb. "Because it's my job?"

"Aren't you just the office girl?"

"No, I'm not just the *office girl*!"

I can tell right away I've insulted her, and I feel bad. "Sorry... I didn't mean it like that. I just thought you were an assistant or something."

She rolls her eyes and starts walking toward the main building. "I was an assistant, for like a year... five years ago when I was starting college."

"And what are you now?"

"I'm the accountant," she says. "And HR. And basically all the hard stuff about running a business that Bruce doesn't know how to do so he pawns off on me. I'm the one who created a spreadsheet to calculate the mechanic's paychecks and you, sir, make enough money to buy a new phone."

I snort. I'm the lead mechanic, so I do get paid more as a base salary. Plus we're paid a set amount for each type of job we do. Like her, I started working here as a kid just out of high school, and Bruce paid for me to become a licensed motorcycle mechanic. I've worked my way up in this little company and I'm proud of it. In fact, I've talked with Bruce about taking over the business when he retires one day. If someone had called me just a shop hand, I'd be insulted, too.

"I'm sorry," I say again as I walk next to her. "I didn't realize you were the accountant. I never really see the office people. I'm Cody."

"I know," she says, giving me the slightest grin. "I write your paychecks, remember?"

"Right..." I say. She turns left toward the back entrance to the main building. I have no more reason to follow her since my shop is in the other direction. "Well, it was nice chatting with you, Miss Katy the accountant."

She snorts. "Get a new phone."

I stand here a moment and watch her walk

inside. She's prettier than I realized. I guess I never really paid attention to the girls who work in the office. The other one, Ari, has a boyfriend. That's obvious because they always eat lunch together in the employee lounge. But Katy is a mystery.

A beautiful mystery.

She's sassy, too, and that's kind of a huge turn on. I look down at my jacked up phone and smile to myself before tucking it away in my pocket and turning toward the workshop. After that encounter just now, the old me would have wanted to ask Katy out on a date.

But not anymore. I'm done with dating. Been there. Done that. I have two broken engagements to show for it. And now I've fully learned my lesson and have decided I won't be dating anymore. Maybe not ever again. Katy might be gorgeous and I can already see myself getting lost in those dark brown eyes for hours... but I won't let it come to that.

She's just a woman at work.

Yep. Just a woman at work. She's a coworker, no different than any other guy who works on bikes in the shop with me.

The more I say it to myself, the quicker I'll believe it.

CHAPTER 3

Katy

Technically I have my own office at work. Behind the main motorcycle showroom, down a hallway marked Employees Only, are four offices. Bruce has the biggest office which also has several windows that look out at the road, which isn't much of a view but it's still a view. The next office is empty and used as storage for office supplies and the last two offices are mine and Ari's. We're across the hallway from each other and we used to open our doors so we could lean forward and see each other when we needed to talk.

Bruce hired Ari to be Zee Cycles' social media manager, a position he only heard about on a Facebook ad and decided he needed to have immediately. Ari is a few years younger than me and full of energy.

She's something of an influencer herself with her makeup Instagram page. The girl is gorgeous, and even though she's plus-sized, she doesn't let it bother her confidence one bit. I wish I could say the same, but I'm always stressing over my huge butt or the flab on my arms.

Anyway, Ari is beautiful and a talented makeup artist, and if we didn't work together I'd probably think she's got way too much energy to be my friend. But we do work together, and now she's one of my favorite people. Which is probably why we don't have separate offices anymore. Technically, we do. But a few months ago, we got tired of talking through our doors and across the hallway, so Ari rolled her office chair into my office, set her laptop up on the other side of my massive wooden desk, and started working that way.

I probably don't get as much work done as I used to, but it's more fun this way.

Ari is a few minutes late to work this morning and I'm anxiously tapping my foot on the floor when she finally arrives.

"Sorry I'm late," she says, shimming into my office with two large coffees from Brew, the best coffee shop in town. "Cinnamon peppermint white chocolate latte," she says, setting the coffee down in front of me.

It's my favorite holiday drink and Brew only makes them from Thanksgiving day until the new year. I cup my hands around the warm drink that smells like Christmas and perfection. "You are totally forgiven for being late," I say, taking a sip. "I mean, how dare you for making me wait to tell you gossip."

Ari's eyes go wide and she drops into her chair with a sharp thunk. "Gossip? Where is this gossip? Tell me the gossip now, girl!"

I chuckle, taking another sip of my latte. "Well, it's not exactly gossip... it's just something that happened."

She flattens her hands on the table, playfully acting over dramatic. "I can't believe you'd hold me in suspense like this after I brought you a coffee!"

I smirk. "Okay, I'll tell you. But it's really not that big of a deal..."

"Spill it, chica!"

"You know that Cody guy who works here?"

"You mean the incredibly hot motorcycle mechanic who is super sexy and mysterious?" She rolls her eyes. "Of course I know him."

"He called me the office girl."

She stares at me for a beat as if she's waiting for me to continue. "And?"

"He called me the office girl!" I say, putting a little more indignant outrage into my voice. "Office girl? How rude is that? First of all, I'm a woman, not a girl..."

Ari holds up her hand. "Wait, wait, wait... you talked to that hot mechanic this morning and you're complaining about it instead of swooning over it?" She tosses her hair over her shoulder. "Girl, he can call me anything he wants..."

I roll my eyes. "It's guys like him who think because they're attractive, they don't have to care about anyone else. He just sees me as some *girl* when I'm really the person who keeps this entire business running."

Ari leans forward, elbows on my desk while she cups her chin, watching me with enthusiasm. "Oooh, girl you've got it bad for him."

I roll my eyes and start checking my email so I don't have to meet her gaze. "You are ridiculous. I do not like him. I've never even cared about his existence until I ran into him today, but if anything, now I hate him."

"Sure," she says, her voice dripping with sarcasm. "I *totally* believe you."

"I'm about to kick you out of my office," I say, trying to make a serious face but not succeeding. "You're supposed to be on my side."

"I am on your side, always." She puts a hand to her chest. "I will stop talking about Mr. Mechanic McDreamy if it makes you happy."

"Yes, please. No more talking about that jerk."

She pretends to zip her lips closed, which is futile, even in an imaginary sense because the girl does not know how to be quiet. Case in point, two seconds later she's talking again.

"So, do you have a date to the Christmas party yet?"

I groan. "No. I told my grandma I'd bring her as my date and she said no."

"Ouch," Ari says, wincing. "Rejected by your own grandma."

I laugh. "She wants me to find a real date. As if I could find a real date by this weekend! It's impossible."

"Well..." Ari tilts her head in thought and I hold up a finger.

"Don't even think of saying it."

"Oh, I'm thinking it," she says, wiggling her eyebrows.

"I'm not asking Mechanic Dreamy-face or whatever you called him to be my date. That's not happening. Never in a million, billion years."

She takes a sip of her coffee. "Fine. Fine. I'll shut up. I do remember what it's like to be single though, and I feel for you. It's not fun."

Despite our light-hearted banter just a few moments ago, I'm suddenly hit with a sadness that feels bone-deep. "I hate being single," I mutter. "But I don't know how to meet guys, either. I'm out of school and I live in a small town. There's nowhere to meet new guys. All the guys I know are just guys I grew up with in school and I've known them so long it's like we're all family. Sterling is such a small town, there's never anyone new to meet."

"Okay, but there are several other towns around here, ya know," she says, peering at her phone. Being on the company social media pages all day is part of her job, so it's not rude when she talks to me while typing on her phone. "All you have to do is get out and meet someone. Teddy lives in Lawson, which is only twenty minutes away."

Ari's boyfriend Teddy is a professional gamer. It might sound weird, but he actually earns decent money playing video games online for his hundreds of thousands of fans who subscribe to his YouTube channel. The two of them make an adorable couple.

They invite me out to hang out with them all the time, but sometimes I'll have to make up an excuse and say I'm busy because being around such a perfectly adorable couple can really make me feel sorry for myself sometimes.

"How did you meet Teddy?" I ask. "And does he have any older single brothers?"

She snorts. "His brothers are sixteen-year-old twins, so no, sorry. But Teddy and I met through speed dating." Her eyes widen. "You should totally find a speed dating event!"

"A *what*? I didn't even know that was real... I thought speed dating was like some joke on TV shows."

She shakes her head. "Nope, it's real. I was just chilling at the mall one day and saw a speed dating event taking place and I thought it'd be fun. Didn't realize I'd meet my soul mate."

My teeth dig into the inside of my lip, and I can't even believe I'm allowing my brain to entertain this idea but... maybe speed dating would be kind of cool? I'd get to meet several guys in one day and maybe one of them would end up being pretty awesome, just like how Ari met Teddy.

"It's really fun," Ari says, setting her phone down and turning to her laptop. "Let's Google...."

After a few moments, she frowns. "Dang, I can't find any speed dating events around here. There's one in like, eight months at some country club an hour away."

Chills prickle over my skin. "I think I just had an idea..."

Ari's eyes flash with excitement. "Do tell..."

"Well, remember how Bruce rented the pavilion for the Christmas party? He actually has it reserved for three days because he wanted a day to set up and another day to take down the decorations. Apparently last time his wife threw some fundraiser banquet thing, it took much longer than they'd anticipated so he wanted more time with this party."

"Oh my gosh," Ari says. "We have the pavilion for three days?"

I nod.

"We can totally do our own speed dating event!"

I nod again. "I wonder if Bruce would mind?"

She sits up straight and takes my phone off my desk, turning it around to face her. "Only one way to find out."

Ten minutes later, Ari and I are bustling around my office, in full on event-planning mode. Bruce was happy to let us use his pavilion rental the day before the party, especially after I promised I'd set up and take down all the decorations so he'd have nothing to worry about. We have a little less than a week to plan and host the speed dating event, but Ari assures me that she's trained her entire life for this moment. She's a social media influencer, after all. She promises she can get lots of people to sign up for it.

Ari and I get to work. I Google everything there is to know about speed dating and start making notes on how to run the event while Ari comes up with a plan to get people to sign up. Usually there's a fee to participate, so we decide to charge a small twenty dollar fee, but then donate all the money to a charity that provides meals for people in need.

The more we work, the more excited I get. Speed dating. It sounds totally ridiculous, but it worked for Ari and now she's with an amazing guy who loves her. In fact, we're all pretty sure he's going to propose to her soon.

And if it worked for Ari. Maybe it'll work for me. Maybe I'll meet a great guy at speed dating and then take him to the Zee Cycles Christmas party the next night.

It's Christmas, after all. Magical things can happen this time of year.

CHAPTER 4

Cody

After a grueling hour of trying to fix this piece of junk motorcycle, I drop my wrench and sit up straight, stretching out my aching back and sore neck. This little rolling stool in my mechanic bay isn't exactly comfortable, and I can easily get lost peering inside a motorcycle's engine while working out the problem. My neck and back aren't too pleased with me right now.

I stretch out my arms, holding them up toward the dusty metal rafters in the ceiling. Overhead, loud rock music plays through the speakers. Ricky's turn to pick the music today. I'm not a fan, but I'll get him back tomorrow when it's my turn to choose the music.

I wring out my hands, stretch my neck from left

to right, and then get back to work. Vintage motorcycle repairs aren't exactly my favorite part of the job, but they pay well. You can't trust just anyone to repair a 1950 Norton Manx, but you can trust me.

After making some good progress, I decide it's time for a break. From the motorcycle and from the awful head-banging, thrashing, no-melody-what-so-ever music. There's a fridge out here in the shop but it's empty, and I could really use a Dr. Pepper, so I grab the flattest dollar bill in my wallet and make my way across the building toward the main show room with the good vending machines. Only they're also out of Dr. Pepper. Lots of orange soda, but none of what I want. My last hope is in the break room in the main office. I rarely go in there because it's all shiny and clean and mechanics are dirty and smell like grease.

As soon as I turn the corner and enter the nice break room, I smell that same floral perfume that I smelled this morning. And there she is, the beautiful office girl. Accountant, I correct myself. The woman who sees my paychecks.

Her back is to me so she doesn't notice me come in. I walk to the vending machine, grateful that its supply of Dr. Pepper seems full, and slip my dollar into the slot.

The office accountant looks over at me, blinking as if I'm the last person she expected to see.

"Hello again," I say, bending to get my soda.

"Hi." She turns back to the bulletin board on the wall, then places two pushpins into a flyer.

I glance over and read it. I must make a face or something because she puts her hands on her hips. "What?"

"Nothing."

She glares at me.

I shrug. "Speed dating?"

"You don't have to say it all judgmental-like."

I hold up my hands innocently, the cold Dr. Pepper in one of them. "I'm not judging...Wait... are you planning on going to this thing?"

"I'm actually hosting it. And yes."

"You're hosting a speed dating event?"

She nods, the fierce look on her face almost daring me to poke fun at her for it. But I really want to poke fun of her for it. I mean, she's a beautiful woman. Why does she need speed dating? All she has to do is walk up to any man and say hello and they'll instantly fall in love.

"That's... cool," I say, suddenly too flustered to think of anything normal to say.

"It's actually not as stupid as it sounds," she says,

her shoulders relaxing a bit. "This is a small town and it's hard to meet people and this event helps fix that problem. And it's easy because you only have to spend sixty seconds with each person, so if you don't like them, then it doesn't matter."

"So what happens if one of the guys likes you but you don't like him?"

"It's set up like those dating apps, only in real life. We each get a card with everyone's name on it. We can put a check next to the names we like, and then at the end of the event, everyone turns their cards in and I'll let everyone know which of the matches they got. So if you like someone but they don't like you back, you don't get their email address. But if you do like someone and they like you, then you both get each other's email."

"Why email and not phone numbers?" I ask.

"That was Ari's idea," Katy says. "It's safer to use your email. I mean, what if someone is a stalker or something? You don't want them to have your real number until you know them better."

"That's so romantic," I say, my voice dripping with sarcasm.

"Oh hush." She turns on her heel. "If you don't like it, you don't have to go."

"Good," I say with a grin as she glances at me

while walking out of the break room. I'm not gonna lie, my knees feel a little weak when she looks at me like that. I swallow and tell myself to let it go. She's just a coworker.

Right after she leaves, Bruce walks into the breakroom whistling an old Metallica song.

"Oh, hey Cody," my boss says, clapping a hand on my shoulder. "Fancy running into you here."

"The other machines are out of Dr. Pepper," I say, feeling out of place in my jeans and T-shirt next to my boss and his dry-cleaned gray suit.

"I was just about to go talk to you, so you saved me some trouble by already being here."

"Oh yeah?" I ask, hoping he's got another awesome project for me like the last time he made the trek out to my bay to see me at work. He'd given me the bones of a 1999 Harley Davidson Heritage Softail Classic and told me I could keep it.

"Yeah, so Katy and Ari are setting up some event thing at the pavilion I rented the day before the Christmas party."

"The speed dating thing," I say, nodding toward the flyer on the wall. "I heard about it."

"Great, well you're going to go help them set up and take down the decorations."

"I'm going to what now?" I say, hoping I heard him wrong. I'm a mechanic. I don't do stuff like this.

"I'll pay your overtime rate," he says, giving me a hearty smack on the back as he goes to fill up his coffee mug. "Thanks, Cody. I can always count on you."

Guess I will be going to speed dating after all.

CHAPTER 5

Katy

Together, Ari and I come up with the perfect theme for our speed dating event: The Christmas Cupid. It might sound a little strange, but since it's a romantic event, we're combining the Christmas holidays, with the spirit of Valentine's day. Plus, it helps that we found a ton of brand new Valentine's decorations in the storage room at work.

The pavilion my boss has rented for his Christmas party is the most gorgeous facility in Sterling. It's right on the water, with a long outdoor boardwalk that overlooks Lake Sterling, and a gorgeous ballroom inside that has floor to ceiling windows that overlook the lake as well. The facility is already decorated for Christmas, so all we have to do is add our pink and red hearts and cupid decorations.

It might end up being a little tacky having both holidays in one room, but I don't care. I am so excited for speed dating. Ari is confident that we can get fifty men and fifty women to show up, which means I'll have fifty chances of finding a date.

And maybe a soul mate?

I know it might sound ridiculous, but what's so bad about hoping to meet my soul mate at a cupid-themed Christmas speed dating event? Stranger things have happened. It would make the most adorable story to tell my future grandchildren one day.

I don't think I ever appreciated Ari's social media prowess until now. I used to think she spent her days taking photos and scrolling through social media, but she does so much more than that. While I'm setting up a website with all the information on our speed dating event, she's working her magic. Once the website goes live, Ari blasts it out into the World Wide Web, targeting all the local social events accounts she already has good relationships with.

The Sterling Chamber of Commerce posts about our event, as well as the South Texas Small Business Association, and a dozen other local organizations. The graphics she made to advertise our event are spectacular. They're filled with Christmas cheer, little cupids and hearts, and all the information someone would need to sign up for our event.

Just two hours after the website goes live, I check our registrations and we're up to forty people.

"Forty people!" I practically shout to Ari who is sitting just an arm's length away.

Her eyes widen. "Nice!"

I log into the website and look through the names as each person registers. I pause on the men's names, wondering if each one might be my potential soul mate. Ricky, is it you? Maybe you, Mathew? Or is it Clay? Guess only time will tell.

As exciting as it is to watch the registrations come in, we do have work for Zee Cycles to do as well, and the last thing I want is for my boss to get upset that I'm neglecting my real job for a fun side thing that he's technically paying for since he's letting us use his rented pavilion space for free. So I dive back into my work, but as soon as the clock reads five, Ari and I clock out and head straight to the pavilion. The Christmas Cupid event is in two days and we need to get started with our decorations.

Ari drives us in her SUV since it's much bigger than my small compact car and we can fit all the Valentine decorations in her car easier. She talks nonstop about how she thinks Teddy will propose to her soon, maybe even on Christmas day.

"Do you want a Christmas proposal?" I ask, knowing some people might not like the idea because it takes away from the holiday.

"Girl, as long as I get two presents, I don't mind," she says with a laugh. "I mean, I want that engagement ring, but it doesn't count as a Christmas present, ya know?"

We both laugh.

"I hope he proposes soon," I say as we arrive at the pavilion. "And I hope you get a ton of presents."

She smiles at me as she chooses a parking spot up close to the doors. "Thanks, Katy. And I hope you find your Prince Charming at speed dating. How many guys have signed up so far?"

"I haven't checked in a while." I take out my phone and log into the website as we walk up the pavilion's decorated cobblestone walkway. I stop short when I see the numbers on my phone.

"Umm..." I say, biting my lip. "I think I made a mistake."

"What do you mean?" Ari says, peering over my shoulder to look at my phone. "Oh wow! We hit one hundred! I mean, I was hoping for fifty but one hundred! Wow!"

"No," I say, shaking my head. "I made a huge mistake. I was supposed to set the website up to stop accepting registrations after we reach one hundred people..." I bite my lip and look up at her. "But I accidently set it for one hundred men *and* one hundred women."

"Wait..." Ari's eyes widen and her mouth drops. "You mean we now have two hundred people registered?"

I take a deep breath. "Yep."

Ari squeals. "This is incredible!"

"No, it's terrible," I say, feeling panic rise up in my chest. "I told the lady on the phone that we needed fifty tables in the event hall, but now we need one hundred or else half the people who show up won't have a place to sit for their speed dating."

Ari waves a hand. Her nails are long and painted in white and red candy cane stripes. "That's not a problem. They have a ton of tables, they're just locked way in this massive storage room. We'll just have to go get them ourselves and set them up like I had to do for my aunt's wedding last year. It'll be fine."

"Are you sure?" I ask.

She nods. "Yep. When you told them how many tables you wanted, that just means how many tables they'll set out for you. But we're strong," she says, flexing her non-existent muscles which makes me laugh. "We've got this, girl. Let's get to work."

"I'm here," a deep voice says from behind us, which makes both of us startle. When we turn around, we find Cody, Mr. Mysterious Mechanic himself, standing there, hands in his pockets. "Where do you need me?"

"Huh?" I say. At least I think that's what I say. My voice kind of makes this weird, surprised sound at the sight of him. He's in crisp clean clothes, dark jeans and a black T-shirt. He must have showered before he came over here.

"Oh great, we need some help," Ari says, opening the door to the ballroom. "Right this way."

Cody follows her lead, glancing briefly at me as he walks by. I swear I think he smirks.

And here I am, still standing here like a deer caught in the headlights.

CHAPTER 6

Cody

"We don't need help," Katy says, flashing me a big smile as she catches up with Ari and me. The smile, while really cute, is totally fake. "You don't have to stay," she adds. "There's not much work to do."

"Are you kidding?" Ari says. "We have a ton of work to do!"

"But we've got it." Katy smiles at Ari then looks at me. "Seriously, you don't have to be here. It's fine."

"I'm on the clock," I say, hoping that helps assuage any guilt she feels over me being here. "Bruce told me to help, so I have to make the boss happy."

"Oh." She frowns. "Well, then fine. We need tables moved if you want to help with that."

"I am at your service," I say. I'm trying to be silly,

by using a fake British accent like I'm a butler or something but she just rolls her eyes and follows Ari across the vast, empty banquet hall.

I guess Katy is still upset that I didn't know she was the accountant. Or maybe she just really hates people with broken cell phone screens. Of course, if I used my phone more than once or twice a day, I might actually buy a new one. But with no girlfriend to text or video chat, what's the point? My phone is basically a device that catches all my family's group chat texts.

I don't know why it bothers me so much that Katy is purposely ignoring me and being short any time she has to talk to me over the next hour. She's *just a coworker*, I remind myself. Only about a dozen people work at Zee Cycles, and a few of them are mechanics like me and we're all close friends. Then there's the salesmen, the service manager, and the office workers. I'm friends with everyone, even Ari, who I rarely see at work. I guess I thought Katy would be just as nice as Ari is to me. But I was wrong.

"Only forty-three tables left," Katy says as she stands next to the storage room, hands on her hips, gazing at the round tables that are stacked high to the ceiling.

"Why do ya'll need this many tables?" I ask, making my way past her to take down more tables. They're stacked three high, which is incredibly unsafe. I don't want either of them to get hurt.

"We have two hundred people signed up for the Christmas Cupid, and with two people to a table, you can do the math," Katy says with a snort. She watches me take down the tables then she reaches for one and starts carrying it out into the banquet hall.

They're small tables, made for just two people to sit at, so they aren't too heavy, but I still wish she'd let me carry them all. I take two, one for each arm, and follow her.

"You had two hundred people sign up for this thing?"

"Yep," she says, briskly walking past me and back to the storage room.

I set my tables down and rush back to her. "Two hundred people are gullible enough to try speed dating?"

She flattens her lips as she stares up at me. "Two hundred people are willing to donate to a good cause and try their hand at finding love. What is so horrible about that?"

"Nothing..." I take the two tables in front of her before she can grab one. "I'm just surprised."

"Well not everyone is a grump like you."

"I'm not a grump," I say, giving her a playful smile. "I'm awesome."

She snorts, taking a table with both hands and starts carrying it out to the banquet hall.

I follow her, setting my tables next to hers. Before I can ask her why she thinks I'm a grump, Ari excitedly rushes to the door and throws her arms around an extremely tall guy with long brown hair.

"Guys, this is Teddy," she says, holding up her hands as if she's presenting him on stage. "He came to help us decorate."

Teddy waves one hand, looking a little awkward to have everyone's attention on him.

"Welcome," I say, waving back across the room. "Good to have you here."

The extra person means we all focus on how best to arrange one hundred tables so that people can move from one table to the next for the event. I don't get to talk to Katy much, which is no fun. I know she's annoyed every time I talk to her, but I keep thinking I might be able to change her mind.

Once the tables are set up, the girls go out to the car to bring in some decorations. I hang out with Teddy, who I've actually met a few times around the shop. He's got a moped he brings in for oil changes every so often.

Teddy's eyes brighten when he sees some kind of module on the wall. "Oh snap," he says, walking over to it. He presses some buttons and soon Christmas music is playing from overhead.

When Ari and Katy walk back inside, their hands full of bags from the party decoration store, Ari's eyes light up. "This is my favorite Christmas song!"

She drops the bags right there on the floor and then holds out her hands to Teddy. "Dance with me, babe."

He obliges. It's that famous Mariah Carrey song that I've heard eight hundred million times in my life, but while Ari and Teddy dance to the music, making puppy eyes at each other and giggling, having a fun carefree time, I realize the song isn't so annoying after all. It's actually kind of fun.

I look over and find Katy standing at one of the tables, slowly rolling strips of tape into a loop to press to the back of cardboard hearts. She's watching her friends with a look in her eyes that seems to mimic the feeling in my own heart. Longing.

I walk over to her. "You want to dance?"

She stiffens. Her cheeks flush a bright pink as she looks up at me. I hold out my hand in earnest, expecting her to take it. I don't really know much about dancing, but when I see how much fun Ari and Teddy are having, I want to have the same kind of fun.

Katy rolls her eyes then peels off another strip of tape, diligently going back to her work. "Oh *ha, ha,* very funny."

I lower my hand, trying to shrug it off like it was a joke.

Maybe breaking through Katy's cold exterior will be harder than I thought.

CHAPTER 7

Katy

I'm so nervous I can't think straight. I haven't been on a date in a couple of years, so it's natural to be nervous for one date. But I technically have one hundred dates tonight. They'll all last just sixty seconds, but still. That's one hundred first impressions. One hundred chances to find love. One hundred chances to say the wrong thing and mess it all up.

I'm nervous for all the normal reasons people get nervous before a first date, but I'm also nervous in a new way. It's an exciting sort of nervousness because I am just totally positive I'm meeting my soul mate tonight. Think about it. The average person doesn't date one hundred guys before they fall in love. Most of my friends got married after a handful of serious boyfriends. My own parents were high school sweethearts who got married after college. They only had one relationship before knowing they'd met the one.

I'm having one hundred one-minute-long dates tonight. Surely my soul mate is in the crowd. Tonight will be extra special. The anticipation is making all the butterflies in my stomach throw themselves an anxious dance party.

Christmas songs play from the living room while I get dressed in my bedroom. We love holiday music around here. Grandma is working on her annual Christmas bake-fest where she makes a ton of cookies and baked goods and then packages them up all cute with ribbons and tinsel to give away to friends and family. The whole house smells amazing but I haven't snuck into the kitchen to steal bites of cookie dough like usual since I'm scared to eat anything tonight. My nerves are already on over drive and the last thing I need is to get so nervous I puke in front of my soul mate.

I'll eat a huge meal *after* speed dating, thank you very much.

"Well," I say as I walk into the kitchen. I hold out my arms and do a little spin. "How do I look?"

Grandma smiles at me. Her apron is smudged

with flour and chocolate icing. "You look absolutely beautiful."

"Are you sure?" I say, patting a hand over my hair. "I'm not overly dressed up?"

"There's no such thing as being overly dressed up," she says as she stirs cookie batter with a spatula. "Everyone else is just underdressed."

I laugh and it calms my nerves a bit. I do look pretty great. Better than normal, at least. I'm wearing a dark green sweater dress with black tights and black high heel boots. A long silver necklace adds some sparkle, and I put way more effort into my makeup and hair styling than I ever do for normal days. Ari and I got manicures after work today, so my nails are painted a shimmery Christmas gold color.

I am ready to meet my true love.

And then tomorrow, I'll bring him to my work's Christmas party, which means I'll get dressed up all over again. It's going to be amazing and full of Christmas wonder.

I can't wait.

The parking lot is still empty when I arrive an hour early since I'm the host of tonight's event, and although that's how it should be—people don't need to arrive early for a timed event after all—I am filled with worries that no one will show up. But the hour passes before I know it, and Ari is here, and we've set up all the tables, prepared the cards for each guest, and set the radio to a Christmas station. Then everyone arrives, all two hundred singles dressed up and ready to meet their dates.

Speed dating is about to happen.

Ari hands me the wireless microphone which is connected to the banquet hall's overhead speakers.

"Good afternoon," I say. My voice booms through the room. Everyone turns to watch me as I stand here on the small podium at the front of the room. All one hundred tables and chairs are arranged in a circle around the room, with numbers at each one, as well as a pink bouquet of carnations as a centerpiece.

"My name is Katy and I'm the host of tonight's Christmas Cupid speed dating event."

I'm not expecting people to cheer at this comment, but they do. Off to the side of the podium, Ari stands, smiling wide as she gives me a thumbs up. I try to glance over the crowd of people, seeing if I can spot some attractive guys who might be potential soul mates, but everything happens so quickly, and it's kind of a rush emotions being up here with so many eyes on me, so it's hard to focus.

I explain how the night will go, then I introduce Ari, who is in charge of the sixty-second timer tonight. She takes my place at the podium, and I go to the first table.

"Let the speed dating begin!" Ari says with a flourish of her hand as she hits the button on the timer.

The man in front of me is tall and lean, with dirty blonde hair and a light sprinkling of freckles on his cheeks.

"Hi there," he says, smiling a toothy grin at me. "I'm Alex."

"I'm Katy," I say, smiling back. It's weird, because it's only been three seconds, but I already know Alex isn't my soul mate. I just don't feel a connection with him. But I tell myself to consider this an opportunity to become a better conversationalist, and soon the timer is going off and Alex moves on to the next table.

Trevor takes his place.

Then Mike.

Then a few other guys, another Mike, and one guy who says he's not comfortable telling anyone his name until he gets to know them. As the sixty-second clock buzzes and resets several times, I find myself getting sore cheeks from smiling so much, and becoming bored from answering the same questions. After forty speed dates, I decide to cut to the chase.

The next guy sits down and reaches out to shake my hand. "Hello, I'm Benjamin."

"I'm Katy, and I'm twenty-six and I've lived here in Sterling my entire life. I work as an accountant at a local motorcycle shop."

His eyes widen. "Wow, do you always talk so much?"

I shrug one shoulder. "I'm just getting all the basic stuff out of the way."

He chuckles. "Sure, I get it. It gets boring repeating the same stuff to a new stranger every sixty seconds. Speed dating is kind of weird."

I nod. "It's fun, though. But everyone asks the same exact questions."

He presses his index fingers to his lips. "Well then, let me think of something interesting to ask..."

It's a breath of fresh air to have something new to talk about. I begin to look him over, mentally appraising if he's soul mate material. He's stocky, with tanned skin and dark hair that's thinning at the temples. He's dressed well, in a charcoal gray sweater and khaki pants.

"Do you like wrestling?"

"Um... the sport?"

He nods. "Well, the professional sport which is totally fake, but also the most amazing sport on the planet."

I lift an eyebrow. "I guess I've never thought much about it."

"Oh, you're missing out, Katy. Wrestling is life. Me and my bros go to every single event in Houston, and we have watch parties twice a week."

Just like that, my slight interest in the man is gone. I'm totally not someone who wants to watch wrestling that much. The timer buzzes and Benjamin moves to the next table. I do not put a check next to his name on my card.

Ten more speed dates go by.

Then ten more.

So far, no soul mates have sat at my table. But I refuse to give up hope that my perfect man is here tonight, waiting to meet me. But even if my soul mate isn't here, surely there is someone good enough to be my date to the work Christmas party tomorrow. I can't show up alone for the fifth year if a row. I just can't.

The banquet hall isn't exactly quiet, since there are two hundred people in here, but suddenly it gets very, very loud. Then the commotion takes over the entire room. Two men are yelling at each other, tossing out profanities and looking like they're about to start throwing punches.

A couple other men try breaking up the fight, but it doesn't go so well. Others are starting to freak out. I rush to the podium and find Ari looking just as concerned as I feel.

"What do we do?" she says.

I don't know why the next thought comes to my head. Maybe because I just saw him earlier today. Maybe because he works for Bruce too and he'll have an interest in making sure we don't lose our deposit on the pavilion hall. Or maybe because when I try to think of someone who can break up to angry dudes fighting, I think of the mysterious mechanic.

"I'll call Cody."

CHAPTER 8

Cody

I don't recognize the number calling me, but something tells me to answer it. When I do, the noise on the other end makes it hard to hear the person on the phone.

"Hello?"

"Cody?"

"Uh, yes. Who is this?"

"It's Katy, from work. I'm sorry to bother you but I don't know who else to call."

I look up from my dinner, glancing back toward the pavilion. I hadn't felt like going home once the event started and Ari didn't need me to help set anything up anymore, so I've been eating dinner at Roger's Diner right down the boardwalk.

"What's wrong?" I can hear what sounds like

yelling on the other end of the phone. I stand up, telling my waitress I'll come back to pay for my food in a minute. I've known her my entire life, so she shouldn't be too concerned that I'll bail on what I owe.

"Two guys are fighting at speed dating. Can you get here soon?"

"I'll be there in a minute. Stay away from them so you don't get hurt."

When I arrive, the fight has just turned from yelling into shoving. I rush through the crowd, debating if I should call the police or just try to handle it myself. But both guys are wearing nice clothes, with gelled hair and shiny leather shoes, and they're not brandishing weapons at each other, so I'm thinking I can handle this myself.

"Fellas, what's going on?" I say, inserting myself right between them, putting a hand on each of their chests. One of them, a taller dude, looks angry that I've intervened, but the other one seems relieved. He takes a few steps back.

"Sorry, man," he says, running his hand over his forehead.

"You better be sorry," the tall guy says. He's still huffing and puffing from the adrenaline of the fight as he turns around, wild-eyed as he looks through the crowd. "Where's that chick in charge?"

I follow his gaze and find Katy and Ari in the crowd, both looking horrified. Katy is absolutely stunning in a green dress and black boots. My heart skips a beat and my mouth goes dry. I want to walk over and talk to her. I want to ask her on a date.

Calm down, Cody, I tell myself. *Not cool.*

The tall guy points at Katy. "You need to make him leave. He's a terrible person. He hooked up with my last girlfriend and tried to lie about it."

Katy's face goes white. It's clear she doesn't know what to do, or say. I step forward.

"You're both leaving," I say, gesturing toward the door.

"What?" Tall guy says, face rumpled up in anger.

"Both of you leave or I'm getting the police involved."

"Sure thing," the other guy says. He ducks his head, shoves his hands in his pockets, and quickly walks out of the banquet hall.

"Let's go," I tell the tall guy.

He looks like he's about to object but I stand tall, letting my body language tell him I'm not going to back down from this. You start a fight at a nice event, you're getting kicked out. There are no ifs, ands, or buts about it.

Finally, he sighs and mutters something under his breath before turning and walking toward the door. I follow him all the way outside, watching to make sure both men get in their cars and leave. Luckily, they turn opposite directions down the road, so hopefully they'll both let it go and move on with their lives.

When I return to the banquet hall, everyone is getting settled back at the small tables. The room is a ridiculous mixture of Christmas decorations and Valentine's hearts, but somehow it works well together. The massive room seems smaller with all these people in it, but my eyes are drawn to Katy almost instantly.

She's talking to Ari, who announces that she's about to start the speed dating event again soon, and asking everyone to go sit at the table they were sitting at when the commotion broke out. But now they're down two men, so two of the women will have to sit alone at a table for each round. Katy says she'll sit aside this round, and another woman who had been sitting at a table with one of the guys who got kicked out volunteers to sit out this round as well.

I walk over to Katy after the sixty-second timer

starts. She doesn't notice me approach at first because she's staring at her nails which are a sparkly gold color. I sit down across from her.

"You're not registered so you can't speed date me," she says, rolling her eyes.

I hold up my hands. "This is a friendly sixty-second chat."

She gives me the slightest little smile and I feel like I've broken down one of her many walls.

"Thanks again for helping with that awful situation," she says, glancing across the room to where the fight had happened. "I had no idea what to do."

"Sure you did," I say with a smile. "You called me, and I handled it. Sounds like you knew exactly what to do."

"How did you get here so fast?"

"I was eating dinner next door."

She gasps. "Oh my gosh, I'm sorry. Did you leave your date alone? You need to hurry up and go back."

I shake my head. "Nah. I was eating alone. And I was mostly done eating, so it's no big deal. I'm just glad I was able to get here before things got worse."

"Well, thank you. I really, really appreciate it."

"You can call me any time you need a fight broken up," I say with a grin.

She grins back.

It feels like another one of her walls just cracked. Her eyes meet mine and electricity zaps through the air. I can feel it. I hope she can feel it. Her cheeks turn a little pink and suddenly I know she feels it too. Another wall is gone. Crumbled to dust.

I'm about to reach out and take her hand.

Then the timer buzzes loudly, making both of us jump.

I stand up, taking a deep breath as I pull myself out of the fog I was in just now. Looking into her gorgeous eyes, surrounded by the scent of her perfume—it does a number on a man. Lord have mercy on all the men speed-dating her tonight. They'll probably end up just as foggy and lovestruck as I am.

Wait, did I just think the word *love*?

"I'll let you get to your next date," I say, clearing my throat as I try to gain my composure. And maybe I'm crazy right now, but Katy looks almost... disappointed? Does she want me to stay? Should I ask to stay?

Another man walks over because it's his turn to sit with Katy for the next sixty seconds. I take another step backward, mentally yelling at myself for wishing I could stay. I need to go outside, let the cold wintery air shock me back to my senses. I'm halfway to the door when I hear my name.

Immediately I know it's not Katy's voice, but I turn around expectantly anyway, hoping maybe it is her.

"Oh my gosh!" Jessica says, rushing up to me, one hand over her open mouth. "Cody! I thought I saw you! Wow, it's been forever."

"Hi, Jessica," I say, as I stare into the eyes of my cheating ex-fiancé.

CHAPTER 9

Katy

Tonight is possibly the weirdest night of my life. I've met so many men and none of them have come anywhere close to being someone I'd want to date. And then that fight broke out, which was terrifying. And now I'm down to only twelve speed dates left and I'm really starting to lose hope.

Not to mention Cody is standing in the corner of the room talking to a beautiful woman. At first I was annoyed that he was trying to pick up women at my speed dating event without signing up to be a participant, but now it's pretty clear they already know each other. The woman talks animatedly, touching his arm frequently and then tossing her hair over her shoulder.

She misses an entire sixty-seconds, and the man

who is supposed to be her date for this minute just sits at the table awkwardly. I don't know what to do, and it's a struggle to pay attention to my date while I'm worried about that poor guy who is dateless for as long as this woman talks to Cody. When the timer buzzes, I jump up and run over to Ari, quickly telling the next guy in line that I'll be right back.

"Hey," I whisper to her as she resets the sixty-second clock. "See that woman over there talking to Cody? She missed her last date because she's talking to him. Can you go over there and make her get back to her table or something? I feel bad for the guy sitting at her table."

"Sure thing," Ari whispers back.

I thank her and then rush back to my table, apologizing to the man sitting there. Ari starts the timer and our sixty second date begins.

"So what made you want to host a speed dating event and also participate in it?" my date asks. He's handsome, with dark skin and kind eyes.

"Wow, we've had ninety-something dates tonight and that's the first time I've been asked that question," I say.

He smiles, lacing his fingers together on top of the table. "I'm Andre, by the way."

"I'm Katy," I say. "Well, I guess I really wanted to

find a boyfriend, and my friend met her boyfriend at speed dating... so we decided to host our own speed dating."

"You're a go-getter," he says with a nod. "I dig that. So, how's it going so far? Do you have a bunch of check marks?"

He's talking about our cards with all one hundred dates on it. I glance across the room and see Ari sheepishly trying to cut into the conversation between Cody and that woman. Ugh, Cody. This is his fault. He shouldn't even be here, and now he's monopolizing the company of one of my guests. I'm glad he broke up that fight, but now he needs to leave.

Andre clears his throat. "Is something wrong?" he says, following my gaze to the other side of the room. His voice jars me back to the present.

"Sorry, no," I say, remembering the question he'd asked me. "I actually don't have many check-marks," I say with a frown. "Maybe I'm being too picky."

"Nah, it's good to be picky," he says. "If the goal in life is to be happy, you should only settle for what makes you happy."

"That's good advice." I decide right here that I'm going to put a check by Andre's name. He's the only guy who's had anything unique to say this whole evening.

As the last few dates go by, Ari is having a terrible time trying to make the woman go. Cody even shakes his head a few times, takes a few steps back, and looks uncomfortable. I can't hear what they're talking about from this far away, but I slowly stop blaming Cody for ruining this woman's speed dating evening. It's clear he's trying to make her go back to her table and she's the one refusing.

I try to shove aside my anxiety. The night is almost over. In fact, when the timer goes off again, we're down to the very last date. Date number one hundred. As embarrassed as I am by the fight that broke out, and as annoyed as I am that this woman is avoiding her last few dates to talk to Cody, at least it's almost over.

Ari starts the timer for the last time and a man sits down in front of me. He smells like he dumped half a bottle of cologne over himself tonight, and while the cologne itself isn't a bad smell, it's so over-powering it's hard to breathe.

"I'm going to level with you," he says, shoving his blonde, unkept hair over his eyes. He reaches into his blazer and pulls out a ring box. When he opens it, a solitaire diamond ring sits inside.

"I'm thirty years old and I've been single most of my life. I'm tired of waiting, and I'd like to get married."

I stare at him. "You're not seriously proposing right now?"

He shrugs. "Why not? It would make a great story. Take this ring and we'll drive out to Vegas tonight and elope."

"You don't even know my name."

He grins. "What's your name, gorgeous?"

I try not to throw up. "Have you proposed to every woman tonight?"

"Only the hot ones," he says, pushing the ring closer to me. "And you're pretty hot."

"No, thank you." I push the ring box back across the table. "I'm not looking to marry someone I don't even know."

He spends the next forty-five seconds trying to convince me to rethink my answer to his ridiculous proposal. When the timer goes off, I've never been so happy to hear an annoying buzzing sound in my life.

CHAPTER 10

Cody

I'm not the kind of person to cause a scene. In fact, I hate scenes. And now I am unwillingly in the middle of what can only be called *a scene*. Jessica refuses to go back to her table for the rest of speed dating, and when I try to leave, she grabs my arm and won't let go. I don't want to draw the attention of everyone else in this room, so I'm stuck trying to quietly and calmly convince her to leave me alone.

That annoyingly loud sixty-second timer keeps going off and before I know it, Ari is announcing the end of speed dating.

"You've missed the rest of the event," I tell Jessica.

"Who cares?" she says, making a snooty face

toward the tables. "You're here and you are the only person I want to talk to."

I have a sudden memory of how many times I've seen that snooty face of hers in my life. Her lips are the signature red lipstick, always pursed into some kind of disapproving frown or look that says she thinks she's better than everyone else in the room. It makes me wonder why I ever dated her in the first place. I was hurt when she cheated on me and ruined our relationship, but now that it's in the past, I can see it was for the best that we broke up.

"The event is set up for one man and one woman. Without you, it's uneven."

"It was already uneven because of those idiots who got in a fight," she says with a snort. "Come on, Cody, let's go get coffee and ice cream and hang out."

"That's not happening."

"Why not?" she says so loudly, I cringe. "We haven't seen each other in a few years, and now suddenly we're here at the same time! That's a sign."

"It's a coincidence, and that's all it is."

She shakes her head. "You have to talk to me. Come on, Cody. You shut me out last time and you never let me explain anything."

"There is nothing to explain."

People are walking around now, chatting and

milling about. I'm feeling so uncomfortably hot for some reason, probably because all the annoyance I have over my ex basically cornering me and making me talk to her is warming me up.

"I'm leaving," I say, turning on my heel. Now that the event is over, I can walk away. I don't have to keep talking to her just to be polite.

"Cody, wait!" Jessica rushes, hobbling on extremely high heels as she catches up with me. She grabs my arm to steady herself. "I'm not letting you walk away from me."

"I didn't ask your permission," I say, trying to slip out of her arm but she's got an iron grip on me.

She follows me all the way outside. As the Christmas music fades, left behind in the banquet hall, the sounds are replaced by a cold breeze rustling through the trees. I'm exhausted. This has been a weird week that played with my emotions, and the last thing I need right now is to be dealing with my ex.

"I'm going home," I say, finally pulling out of her grip.

"No, you're not!" Jessica says. "You're so immature! Why can't you just stop walking for five seconds and talk to me!"

I stop, turning to her, my jaw set. I'm not trying to be rude but she's really getting on my nerves.

"There is nothing to talk about," I say slowly, so she hears every word. "You and I broke up a long time ago, and now I don't want to see you or talk to you. We're done."

"It was a long time ago," she says, her eyes pleading with me. "I've changed. I'm different now. And I really miss you and I want to see you. Where are you working now?"

I snort. Like I need her showing up at my place of work unannounced. No, thank you.

"Bye, Jessica."

"Cody, you're being such a jerk!"

"If I'm being a jerk, it's because you've refused to accept all the polite times I asked you to leave me alone and now I'm running out of patience."

"I just don't understand why you won't take me back. We were so good together."

I quirk an eyebrow. "You cheated on me."

"So what, that was so long ago!" She pokes out her bottom lip. "I miss you, Cody. You were the best thing that ever happened to me. You spoiled me and you gave me everything. I haven't found another guy like you, and I miss you. Please take me back."

My teeth grind together. Here is she praising me.

I seem to remember all the complaints she had about me back when we were together. She thought I spent too much time studying in school. She hated motorcycles. She hated that I didn't want to film live videos of our dates for her social media. I was only twenty-three back then. I was young and dumb and I tried so hard to make her happy without ever stopping to decide if she made me happy.

I tried this the nice way, but I guess the nice way doesn't always work.

"I'm sorry, Jessica. But you and you alone ruined the relationship we had when you cheated on me. I've moved on, and I'll never be interested in you again. Goodnight."

I can feel her glare boring into my back as I walk away, but she doesn't follow. I make it to my truck and I'm about to drive home, before remembering I still need to pay my bill at Roger's Diner. On the short drive back to the restaurant, I can't stop remembering that relationship I'd had with Jessica. It wasn't good. It wasn't happy. I tried so hard back then, and I don't even know why. I've spent years after the fact thinking I didn't want a relationship because it would just fall apart the way my previous relationships had crumbled and erupted.

But I just spent two days around the most

amazing woman. Katy doesn't seem fake. She doesn't pretend to be nice and then be rude behind your back. She's just herself, through and through. Sure, she's got walls built up, but maybe she placed them there for a reason. Maybe she's been hurt in the past, too.

Maybe there's a way forward for both of us. Maybe the Christmas Cupid didn't shoot an arrow into Katy tonight, but I'm starting to think he shot one into me.

CHAPTER 11

Katy

I owe Ari all my gratitude. The moment the final timer went off, she took the microphone and wrapped up the event perfectly, letting everyone know they'll be emailed their matches within twenty-four hours and thanking them for attending and for their payment which went to charity. We hadn't discussed how we'd wrap up the event before it started, but she's done it perfectly. So perfectly that I don't feel bad for rushing straight to the bathroom instead of going up to the podium and helping her end the event.

I go to the staff bathroom at the far end of the hallway so no one will come in here and notice me, and the moment the door closes behind me, I burst into tears. Sobs pour through my body in a flood of emotions. Anger, sadness, defeat. Even jealousy. It's not my place to care about the woman who took Cody away tonight, but my heart still hurts a bit when I think of it. I couldn't stop watching them. I watched them walk all the way out of the room together, her hand holding onto his arm like he's a perfect Prince Charming. Seeing Cody with that woman was the final straw on top of a terrible evening.

I had one hundred dates and all of them were bad. Not a single guy on my card was interesting enough to make me want to see him again. I don't even want to ask any of them to the Zee Cycles party tomorrow. It all just seems so hopeless.

I spent all this time and effort planning an event, selfishly hoping it would score me a date, and a boyfriend, and someone to finally settle down and live life with. Instead, I got nothing. The only consolation is knowing we raised a good bit of money for a local charity. I tell myself to be happy for that much, but it still hurts. I was so hopeful. So confident. Tonight was supposed to be magical and full of Christmas cheer.

Instead, I'm crying my makeup off in an employee bathroom.

When I finally pull myself together, wipe off my

smudged mascara, and walk back to the banquet hall, I'm stunned at what I find. All one hundred tables have been put away. The chairs are stacked and lined up in the storage room. The Valentine's decorations are gone.

"What happened?" I ask. I know I just had a breakdown in the bathroom, but it couldn't have taken longer than thirty minutes. I'd expected everyone to have left by now, so I could clean up the place in silence.

"I got a ton of guys to help out," Ari says with a smile. "I just asked if anyone was strong enough to help move the tables and chairs, and you know how single men are..." She sucks her teeth and grins. "They love showing off. I had like thirty guys in here moving everything back into the storage room and it took no time at all."

She gestures toward the bags at her feet. "I kept the Valentine's stuff. Figured we can hang it up at work when V-day comes around."

"You're the best," I say, pulling her into a hug. Tears threaten to fall again, but this time at least they'd be happy tears. Still, I hold them back. My nose is already stuffy from earlier. I don't feel like crying again.

Ari must sense that I'm bummed out, but she

doesn't say anything. She's great like that. She knows when I feel like talking and when I'd rather be left alone. We walk out to our cars together, and we're the only cars left in the parking lot. I don't know why I'd hoped that maybe Cody had come back to check on us or something. Of course he wouldn't. Bruce only paid him to help set up the decorations, not to help us put them away.

My chest tightens as I think about Cody on my drive home. Tomorrow is our work's Christmas party, which will be filled with all of our clients and many customers, as well as the employees and their dates. Cody will no doubt bring that woman with him tomorrow.

And I'll be stuck standing around awkwardly at a party, all alone.

Merry Christmas to me.

CHAPTER 12

Cody

Katy isn't at work the next day. I've worked at Zee Cycles for years and have never once known if Katy was here or not. It's not something that's ever crossed my mind. I come to work, fix motorcycles, then go home. But today is different. I made up an excuse of needing more printer paper for the old dusty barely working printer in the shop that no one ever uses. I walked all the way to her office only to find it empty.

Ari pokes her head out of her own office when she sees me. "What's going on?"

"Just looking for Katy."

Her expression changes from boredom to extreme curiosity in a fraction of a second. "What for?"

"I need printer paper."

She quirks an eyebrow. "Office supplies are in the office supply room, which is right there." She points to the room in question, the one with a laminated piece of paper on the door that reads: OFFICE SUPPLY ROOM.

I know the room is there, but I pretend I don't.

"Cool, thank you."

"Katy isn't here today," Ari says, leaning out of her office door like she's not quite ready to get back to work.

"Okay."

"She's not sick or anything. She's just busy. She'll be at the party tonight."

Ari watches me with a curious expression, like she's eager to see how I'll react to that. Unfortunately, I think my reaction is pretty telling because she grins. "You like her, don't you?"

"What?"

"Katy. You like Katy."

"I barely know Katy."

She shrugs. "You don't have to know someone to like them. I like Ryan Reynolds and I've never met him."

"I'll just get my printer paper now," I say, ducking into the supply closet to avoid the conversation. I don't really need paper, but I take some anyhow. When I emerge, Ari is still standing there, grinning at me like she knows some deep romantic secret. And I guess maybe she does, because she's asking me something I'm too embarrassed to admit.

I give her a quick wave, then get out of the building and rush back to the safety of my motorcycle bay where no one ever asks me questions about liking my coworkers. It's probably a bit immature of me, but I'm still figuring out what's happened to my life over the last few days. I went from happily being a single man who stays away from relationships to being someone who lies about needing printer paper in the hopes of seeing a girl.

With only one motorcycle to fix today, I finish up work early and head to Roger's Diner for dinner. I'm still on the fence about attending the fancy Christmas party tonight, and while they will have fancy banquet food at the event, it doesn't start until seven. I'm hungry now. Plus, a little burger and fries never spoiled my appetite. I'm always hungry.

I'm making my way to the bar so I can eat alone like usual, but then I see my friend Max sitting at a table, so I figure I'll have dinner with him. Max and I go way back. He's a carpenter and I'm a mechanic so we often trade our skills for each other. He helped me rebuild my back porch last summer and I replaced his brake pads not long ago.

But as I make my way over, I notice a woman emerge from the restrooms and sit down in front of him. She has brown wavy hair and a bright, doe-eyed smile as she looks at my friend. I'm trying to remember how long it's been since I talked to Max. A few months, I guess. I didn't realize he had a new girl in his life. I'm about to turn around and leave him to his date but he notices me and says hello.

"Hey man," Max says. "Happy early Christmas."

"You too," I say. "How's the family?"

"They're good." He holds out a hand toward the woman in front of him. "I don't think you've met Julie yet, have you?"

"Nope," I say, smiling to the woman and reaching out to shake her hand.

"Nice to meet you," she says.

"You here alone?" Max asks, glancing behind me.

"Well, you know me," I say with a chuckle. "I'm always alone."

"You should eat with us," Julie says, removing her purse from the chair in front of me.

Normally I'd say no because I don't want to interrupt their date, but I'm grateful for the excuse to forget about all the thoughts going on in my head for a while. Plus, they seem happy to have me, and it's just Roger's Diner. It's not like they're at a fancy restaurant or anything.

I join them, and I learn all about Max's new girlfriend Julie. She's a romance novelist and even has a TV show coming out soon that's based on her books. Max really hit it out of the park with this girl. It's clear they have a real love for each other, and I'm happy for him.

"You still stubbornly living the single life?" Max asks.

Leave it to this dude to always tell it like it is, not skirting around uncomfortable topics. I take a bite of my burger to avoid the question a bit longer, but then I shrug. "Yeah, for the most part."

Max's eyes go wide. "Uh oh... someone caught your eye?"

"Maybe."

Julie smiles. "That's exciting."

Max shakes his head. "Eh, I'll believe it when I see it. My boy Cody has been avoiding relationships for a while now."

"Well, when the perfect woman for him shows up, he'll know it," Julie says, giving me a kind smile.

I quickly change the subject to sports. Sure, she's right and all. And Max is also right. But talking about my love life is not something I feel like doing, not when all these anxious feelings are rolling around just underneath my rib cage. The thing is, my perspective has changed this week. I've been shut off from the possibility of dating for so long that I didn't even think about it anymore.

And then I ran into Katy and accidentally insulted her job title and now I can't stop thinking about her. Helping out at the Cupid dating thing was fun. More fun than I ever imagined. And then being called in during an emergency to help her out was the best feeling ever. I want to be there for her. I want her to call me for every emergency, big and small.

I want what Max and Julie so clearly have right here in front of me. Real love.

This work party thing tonight is never something that's on the top of my list of things I'd call fun. If anything, it's exactly the opposite. I'm not a big fan of dressing up nice and schmoozing with customers. It's even worse when Bruce likes to show me off as his best mechanic to all of his rich business friends. They're not bad people or anything, it's just... not my scene. I'd rather be home hanging out next to a bonfire or playing football with my nephews. But now that I know Katy will be at the party tonight, it's starting to sound like the only place I want to be.

As I'm walking out to my truck after having dinner with Max and his amazing girlfriend, I decide to make a promise to myself. I'll go to the party. I'll even wear that all-black suit I wore as a groomsmen in my buddy's wedding last summer. The suit everyone kept saying looked amazing on me. I'll find Katy.

Then I'll tell her how I feel. I'll ask her to go on a date with me.

If she says no, then I'll let it go.

But if she says yes...?

It'll be the best Christmas ever.

Katy

My migraine excuse doesn't seem to fool anyone except my boss. He tells me he's so sorry and hopes I feel better soon. But Ari texts me constantly all day, telling me she knows I'm faking and that I better get my butt to the party tonight or else. And Grandma watches her TV shows loudly like usual and invites all her diamond painting friends over to be loud and chatty while they work on their projects in the living room all day. If she'd truly believed that I had a migraine, she wouldn't have done any of that. She'd have pulled all the blinds closed, kept the TV volume low, and doted on me all day until I felt better.

Sure, I'm faking the migraine, but I think I deserve a day off. My heart feels broken, which I know is silly because it's not like I was even dating anyone. But my hopes had been so high that I'd find a man at the Christmas Cupid event, and now it feels like I've been dumped. Not by a man, but by life itself. Am I really going to be a loser who lives with her grandmother forever?

I think I've met every single man in Sterling, Texas and none of them are dateable men. I was supposed to show up at the party tonight with a wonderful, handsome, kind, date.

Instead I've got nothing.

I breathe in a deep breath and then let it out in a deep, soul-crushing sigh. This sucks. I'm still wearing my pajamas even though it's like four in the afternoon, and I've been binge-watching comedy TV shows all day in an attempt to feel better. But I don't feel any better. I just feel pathetic.

Ari texts me again, and I avoid looking over at my phone until it beeps three times in a row. I glance at it—all texts from Ari—but the last one is a bunch of exclamation marks, which piques my interest.

Ari: Girlllllllll

Ari: Hot mechanic totally has the hots for you

Ari: !!!!!!!!!!!!!!!!!!!!!

I quirk an eyebrow. Cody? Why would he have the hots for me? She's probably just texting me crazy things in an attempt to make me respond. Or make me go to the party. Ari is sneaky like that.

I drop the phone on my bed and go back to watching TV. But curiosity is really hard to ignore, and soon I'm calling her.

"What are you talking about?" I ask when she says hello.

"Okay, so, he totally walked in here looking for your office and he was really sad when you weren't here."

"What?" I sit up in bed. Cody never walks down to my office. In all the years I've worked at Zee Cycles, I've never seen him even in my hallway.

"I asked if he liked you—"

"You did *not*!" I interrupt.

She laughs. "Yep, I did. And his cheeks got all red and he left without answering the question. But it's totally obvious he likes you! I could tell last night at the banquet hall. The way he looked at you was so obvious. The man's got it bad for you."

My teeth wear into my bottom lip. I want to accuse her of lying, or of making up things just to trick me. But Ari is a good friend, one of my best friends. She wouldn't lie about this. And she wouldn't tell me her suspicions if she wasn't extremely sure about them.

"You really think he likes me?" I ask, my voice quiet as a million thoughts run through my mind.

"Yep. One hundred percent. And I think you like him, too because no one would have gone on and on about him like you did the other day if you didn't like him."

"Well, he insulted me and I was upset about it."

"People call both of us the *office girls* all the time and you never care," she says.

I draw in a sharp breath, but I can't deny it. She's right.

"He is ridiculously good looking," I admit. "But he seems like a jerk."

"He's *so* not a jerk," Ari says. "He's just got a tough exterior that you could probably crack easily with a snap of your fingers. The guy has got it bad for you."

I sigh.

"You better come to the party tonight, Miss Fake Migraine."

"Maybe," I tease, but deep down I've already made my choice.

I'm going.

Last night had taken me hours to get ready and it was all for nothing. Tonight will be easier because Ari and I are wearing matching Christmas sweaters. They're not of the ugly variety—these are actually really pretty maroon sweaters with silver sparkly snowflakes on the front. It's buttery soft and classy, if there is such a thing as a classy Christmas sweater. I pair it with black skinny jeans and black high heel booties. I curl my hair with a big wavy curl, pinning back my side bangs with a sparkly Christmas hairclip. My manicure still looks great, and I dab on some sparkly eyeshadow and deep red lipstick and then smile at myself in the mirror. I look like a Christmas ornament. But... in a good way. I hope.

I try one last time to convince my grandma to come with me as my plus-one but her arthritis is flaring up so she'd rather stay home. I drive over to the pavilion alone, a nervous excitement running through my veins. The last time I drove here, I was under the impression that I was about to meet my soul mate, one man out of a hundred. Now I'm arriving with a gratitude for my best friend and coworkers, a joyfulness for the holiday spirit that's all around me, and a teensy bit of hope that maybe Ari was right.

She's probably wrong... she probably just thinks that big handsome grouch likes me. But I'm willing to find out for myself. I lose all expectations and just try to let life happen.

I arrive to the party on time, but tons of people are already here. The food spread looks amazing, the Christmas music sounds magical from the live band on stage, and I find Ari dancing with Teddy in the middle of the dance floor. They look so adorable together, so happy and in love, and it warms my heart. I stand off to the side of the room, sipping on a cup of apple cider while I wait for the song to finish so I can hang out with my friends.

One song turns into two, and by the third song, Ari and Teddy are still dancing and I'm feeling a little awkward. I'll end up talking to customers or something soon, and I'm not a fan of small talk. I decide to take the coward's way out of socializing and I refill my apple cider then slip out the side door onto the patio that overlooks Lake Sterling for some peace and quiet. Ari has to stop dancing eventually, and then I'll have someone to hang out with.

A few moments later the door opens, letting out the sound of Christmas music for a few moments before it closes again. I turn around, expecting to see a customer, or maybe Bruce. But it's Cody.

His dark hair is slicked into place. His scruffy beard is trimmed neatly. But it's the suit that takes my breath away. Solid black and form fitting over his lean but muscular body. He's dressed like a celebrity and here I am wearing a sweater and jeans. I feel so underdressed in comparison.

His lips hitch up in a smile as he walks over to where I'm standing at the balcony railing.

"Hi, Katy."

"Hey."

I'm surprised I'm able to utter any sounds, much less a full, complete word, because I'm pretty gob smacked right now. Cody is so handsome in this suit. So handsome in general. And the way he's grinning at me right now feels like new territory.

Good territory.

His tongue wets his lips and then he's standing right in front of me, just a few inches of space between us. I can smell his cologne and see the flecks of gold in his eyes. He's that close.

His eyes meet mine and a little flutter shoots right through my stomach.

"Would it be crazy if I kissed you right now?"

CHAPTER 14

Cody

My heart pounds like a bass drum. My ears start ringing. I can't believe I just said that. It's the last thing I'd ever expect myself to say. I'd driven all the way over here planning out my words very carefully. Precise, poignant words that would let her know how I feel. And then I get here, and I see her, and all rational thought goes out the window and I just blurt out the most insane thing ever.

"Would it be crazy if I kissed you right now?"

"Yes," she says, and my heart shatters. "Yes, it would be crazy."

Her shoulders lift a bit and she grins. "But you can... if you want."

I don't wait a moment longer. I take her cheeks

in my hands and dip my head down to hers. I give myself one brief second to take in her beauty and then I close my eyes and kiss her. The moment our lips touch, my soul ignites. My heart stops pounding like a jackhammer and slips into a smooth rhythm, like this is the place it's been yearning to be.

Katy's lips are soft, her hands delicate as they slide around my neck. She tastes like warm apple cider, and suddenly that's my favorite drink in the world. I want to get lost in her touch, stay here forever. But there's a Christmas party going on just beyond those balcony doors and our boss and several customers are in there. What would they think if they saw us like this?

Slowly, against my own will, I pull back, settling my hands on her waist. I feel dizzy in the best way.

From this close, I can see her eyes are actually a dark green. And there are light freckles spread across her cheeks. She's absolutely beautiful.

"Would you like to dance?" Again, here I am saying things without thinking about it first.

She nods. A cool breeze pours over the balcony, sending a shiver through her. "Maybe inside?" she suggests.

"Let's go." I take her hand and lead her toward the door. "The music is better inside."

Several more people are dancing to the live band now, so it's not awkward as I walk her into the middle of the dancers and then turn to her, saying a little prayer that I'll remember how to dance.

My mom was a dance instructor before she had children, and she taught all of us how to dance when we were growing up. Before my high school prom, she'd twirled and waltzed with me all over the living room to make sure I was prepared for the evening. And then my date stood me up because a more popular guy had asked her to the prom after I did.

"I've never really had a good relationship," I say as I turn to face Katy, slipping my arms around her in the proper dance position. We are the perfect height for each other. She's not too short and I'm not too tall. I can gaze into her eyes with just the tip of my head.

"Is that why you walk around like some big jerk?" she asks, her lips tipped in a tiny smile.

"Maybe," I say. We dance to the music, a semi-slow song that makes for perfect conversation while we twirl around the room. "I don't think I walk around like a big jerk though."

She snorts. "You do. Sometimes."

"Well, I won't anymore. Not with you."

She nods once, accepting my promise. "Go back to the relationship thing you were saying."

"Well..." I don't want to scare her off. I don't want to move too fast and push her away or freak her out. But this needs to be said. I need her to know that I'm all in. "I've had a few...unsuccessful relationships in my life. And I guess it just made me shut down. I haven't wanted to date anyone in a long time, and then I met you and now I can't stop thinking about you."

As the music plays, we get lost in our own little world. I'm only vaguely aware of other dancers around us, of the Christmas classics keeping the beat upbeat and fun. It's almost as if we are the only two people in the room.

She looks down for a moment, and then her eyes rise to meet mine. "I've been thinking about you, too."

"In a good way?" I ask.

She shrugs her shoulders playfully. "I think so."

"I know this isn't a relationship," I say. "Not yet, at least. It's been like thirty seconds. But I want you to know that I'm all in, Katy. I want to take you on dates and spend time with you and treat you the way you deserve to be treated."

"Do you want to stay in Sterling?" she asks.

"What do you mean?"

She swallows and a painful emotion flashes across her face for just a moment. "Like...when you meet your soul mate and you want to live happily ever after—do you want to do that here in Sterling?"

"Of course," I say. "I'd never want to live anywhere else."

Her smile warms me to the core. She squeezes me a little tighter. "Perfect."

"So, are you saying you'll be my girlfriend?"

"Yes..." She tilts her head. "I guess I am saying that. But only under one condition."

I know in this moment that I'm willing to give her anything she asks for. "What's that?"

"You need a new phone."

I laugh. "Consider it done."

The music picks up and I see the perfect opportunity to twirl her around. She gasps when I do, but then she's laughing when I pull her back to me, her back pressing against my chest.

"That was fun," she says, catching her breath. "You're a really good dancer."

She looks up, then her eyes focus on something distracting. I follow her gaze. We're standing underneath a mistletoe. She turns around, pressing her hands to my chest. "We wouldn't want to disappoint the mistletoe," she says.

"No, we can't do that," I say.

Then I pull her in for another kiss.

Sneak Peak of Julie and the Fixer Upper

Chapter One

Romance is for schmucks. You heard me correctly. Romance is for all the people too moon-eyed and stubborn to realize it'll all fall apart in their face one day. Romance gets you nowhere. Snarking on romance, however, will get you *everywhere*.

Assuming you're any good at it.

The navigation app on my phone tells me to turn left. I slow my old Jeep down to a crawl, wondering where exactly the left turn is, finally finding it tucked away in the thick brush of trees that line this old Texas county road. Eyes on the rear-view mirror, I check to make sure the rented box trailer hitched to my car stays there. It's all I have left after my life exploded and I can't lose it. I've never towed anything before, much less all of my precious belongings in an ugly rented box that's not even the least bit aerodynamic. The guy at the rental place warned me not to take sharp turns, so I've spent this entire ten-hour trip worried that the trailer and my Jeep will go tumbling into the ditch each time there's a bend in the road.

So far, so good. And now I'm almost here. Almost *home*.

The last year of my life has been a total disaster. Living in the city didn't help one bit, because when you're in a depressed funk, it's no fun seeing a million other people living their best lives all day long. Who am I kidding? It was no fun seeing *one* person live his best life. In the same apartment complex.

Jason ruined our engagement with his affair, but then he ruined my living situation by shacking up with his new girl in the same downtown apartment complex. Just one hallway over. Then he ruined my career.

It took me ten years to become a recognized name in the romance industry. I poured my soul in to my romance novels, breathing life into my fiction-alized characters, dreaming up swoony romances, and giving my readers couples to root for. I even had a TV network negotiating the rights to adapt my six book city romance series into a cute, romantic television show.

The day I discovered Jason was cheating on me was the day I realized I couldn't write romance anymore. I wanted to. My livelihood depended on the money I get from writing. But I just couldn't. The wool over my eyes had been removed, revealing the truth—that all that sappy, silly romance I had once loved was just a lie.

I shake my head. I won't think about all that I lost. I will only look forward and focus on what I have right now. I catch sight of myself in the rearview mirror and grin. After weeks of looking for the perfect place to live, I finally found it. The GPS says I'm 2.3 miles away from my new home. My dream home.

Butterflies light up in my stomach as I drive down the small road, which is flanked on either side by thick trees. I roll down my window and take in the clean, crisp air. It's a stark difference from the exhaust-filled city air I'm used to. I breathe in deeply, catching sight of my hair in the mirror as it whips around my face.

I had the same boring hairstyle forever, long and straight just like Jason liked it, until a week ago when I got it cut into long layers with light brown highlights to give more definition to my otherwise boring brown hair.

My friends called it a breakup haircut. It's not a breakup haircut, though. It's the haircut a woman gets when she's finally living for herself.

As I drive further down this small road, the thick pine trees part, revealing the hidden beauty of Lake Sterling. The photos online haven't done it justice. It takes my breath away. The afternoon sun glimmers on the deep blue water. The lake is dotted with cottages, all waterfront properties with big back yards, plenty of room around them so you're not too close to the neighbors. I don't need the GPS to find my new home now; I've spent days staring at its picture online.

The white cottage has one bedroom with an extra studio space that I'll use for an office, an open floor plan, and a huge wraparound back porch that faces the water. Little stepping stones lead from the driveway to the front door, and lush, vibrant flowers decorate front of the small home. It is a picture-perfect home. It should be on postcards and puzzles.

I park, trying not to stress about how I'm going to back out of the small gravel driveway with this box trailer attached to my Jeep. I went the entire trip without going in reverse, and I'm not even sure how to take it off the trailer hitch thingy on the back of my car. There's a rental return place located a few miles away in the small town of Sterling, so I'm hoping to unload my stuff and get it turned in tomorrow morning.

My heart races as I step out and stretch my legs, gazing up at the gorgeous place that is now my own for the next two years. Snagging this rental property was a miracle. Sterling, Texas was voted one of the most charming small towns last year, and it shows. The real estate here sells for way more than it would anywhere else, and homes rarely ever come up for sale or rent. The people who live here, love it here.

As much as I loathe my ex, Jason did do something good for me. All the anger and pain I felt during our breakup might have ruined my romance writing career, but it started me on the path to a brand new journey. I was kind of joking when I pounded out an entire anti-romance novel in just fifteen days—a record for me—throwing all my bitter emotions into my made up character, Private Investigator Rosa Ramirez, the man-hating vixen who seeks out and destroys men who cheat on their partners. But my agent loved it and sold it to a publisher just days later—another record for me.

The first book in my Love Sucks series

became an instant bestseller and my publisher wanted me to make it into a series. I just got a massive book advance for the next three books, which gave me the money to plunk down two years' worth of rent at once, which put me in the running to rent my dream home, a small cottage on the lake. I know a dozen other people were hoping to get it, but it's mine now. All mine.

I close my eyes and breathe in deeply, inhaling the sweet scent of the flowers, the crisp spring air, the woodsy pine trees.

"Well, hello, darlin'. What brings you to Sterling?"

The unexpected, somewhat gravelly voice startles me. I yelp, turning around. The woman smiling at me looks to be in her sixties, with bright red lipstick and dark black hair piled into a messy bun on top of her head.

Not everyone in Texas talks like that. I would know, I was born and raised in Dallas and I have never once called someone *darlin'*.

"I'm, uh," I swallow then force a smile and gesture toward my new house. I want to belong here, blend into small town life away from the hustle of the city. Now that I'm here talking to a local, I'm worried she'll know I don't fit in. "I'm new here. I'm moving in today."

"Well then, *welcome*, my dear. I didn't even know the house was ready to be rented!" She holds out her hand. When I go to shake it, she pulls me in for a hug that smells like floral perfume and coffee. "I'm Lina. I live down the road on the left. Blue house, white door. I like to take a walk each evening. Keeps me fit," she says, finally releasing me.

"Nice to meet you."

"I'll let 'cha get back to it," she says, waving as she starts to walk away. "You holler if you need anything, hun."

My landlady lives in Arizona, so we've only communicated through phone and email. She told me the keys would be under a decorative turtle figurine on the back porch. Excitement pulses through me as I make my way across the beautifully green grass yard and into the back yard. I never had a yard in Dallas. It was just concrete as far as you could see.

I step up on to the back porch and gaze out at the lake in front of me. This is stunning. Beautiful. Perfect. I picture sitting out here, sipping coffee and writing my books to the morning sunrise, the sound of birds and nature keeping me company while I fall into my fictional world with P.I. Rosa Ramirez.

I do a little dance on my new back porch. I close my eyes and wiggle and shake, letting loose back here because no one can see me anyway. Just months ago, my life felt like a tragedy. Now I'm thriving. This is my place, in my own little slice of heaven. Jason is a distant memory. In fact, all men are a distant memory.

My dancing is interrupted by the sound of the back door opening.

"Uh... hello?"

My mouth goes dry.

Dirty blonde hair, messy and curly, a scruffy beard, muscles. Muscles for days.

It takes a second for my brain to put all the gorgeous pieces into place, to register that this very attractive man is staring at me, a twist of confusion on his handsome face.

It's only a second, and I'm snapped back to reality. It doesn't matter how good he looks.

There's a man in my house.

About the Author

Amy Sparling is the bestselling author of books for teens and the teens at heart. She lives on the coast of Texas with her family, her spoiled rotten pets, and a huge pile of books. She graduated with a degree in English and has worked at a bookstore, coffee shop, and a fashion boutique. Her fashion skills aren't the best, but luckily she turned her love of coffee and books into a writing career that means she can work in her pajamas. Her favorite things are coffee, book boyfriends, and Netflix binges.

She's always loved reading books from R. L. Stine's Fear Street series, to The Baby Sitter's Club series by Ann, Martin, and of course, Twilight. She started writing her own books in 2010 and now publishes several books a year. Amy loves getting messages from her readers and responds to every single one! Connect with her on one of the links below.

www.AmySparling.com